AXLE ANNIE
AND THE *SPEED GRUMP*

AXLE ANNIE
AND THE *SPEED GRUMP*

Robin Pulver · pictures by Tedd Arnold

Dial Books for Young Readers New York

For school bus drivers everywhere who are dedicated to keeping children safe —R.P.

Specially for Nancy Leo-Kelly —T.A.

———————

DIAL BOOKS FOR YOUNG READERS
A division of Penguin Young Readers Group
Published by The Penguin Group
Penguin Group (USA) Inc., 375 Hudson Street, New York, NY 10014, U.S.A.

Penguin Group (Canada), 10 Alcorn Avenue, Toronto, Ontario, Canada M4V 3B2 (a division of Pearson Penguin Canada Inc.)
Penguin Books Ltd, 80 Strand, London WC2R 0RL, England
Penguin Ireland, 25 St. Stephen's Green, Dublin 2, Ireland (a division of Penguin Books Ltd)
Penguin Group (Australia), 250 Camberwell Road, Camberwell, Victoria 3124, Australia (a division of Pearson Australia Group Pty Ltd)
Penguin Books India Pvt Ltd, 11 Community Centre, Panchsheel Park, New Delhi - 110 017, India
Penguin Group (NZ), Cnr Airborne and Rosedale Roads, Albany, Auckland 1310, New Zealand (a division of Pearson New Zealand Ltd)
Penguin Books (South Africa) (Pty) Ltd, 24 Sturdee Avenue, Rosebank, Johannesburg 2196, South Africa
Penguin Books Ltd, Registered Offices: 80 Strand, London WC2R 0RL, England

Library of Congress Cataloging-in-Publication Data
Pulver, Robin.
Axle Annie and the speed grump / Robin Pulver ; pictures by Tedd Arnold.
p.   cm.
Summary: Always impatient and driving too fast, Rush Hotfoot learns
the importance of safety from school bus driver Axle Annie and her bus full of kids.
ISBN 0-8037-2787-9
[1. Traffic safety—Fiction. 2. Automobile driving—Fiction. 3. School buses—Fiction.]
I. Arnold, Tedd, ill. II. Title.
PZ7.P97325Ay 2005 [E]—dc22   2004022937

The artwork was prepared with colored pencils and watercolor washes.

Special thanks to Milton Saylor —R.P.

Axle Annie was the best school bus driver in Burskyville. She loved the kids, and the kids loved her. Riding on her bus was one of their favorite parts of the day.

But Annie and the kids had a problem, and that problem had a name: Rush Hotfoot.

On his way to work in the morning, Rush Hotfoot was always in a hurry and in a bad mood. He would do anything to avoid slowing down for Axle Annie's bus.

"Watch out for Rush Hotfoot, Annie," the kids would say each morning.

And each morning her reply was the same: "I've got two hands on the wheel and nerves of steel. I always watch out for that speed grump!"

Annie's kids watched out for him too. They watched while Annie drove up, up, up Tiger Hill.

They watched while they sang their favorite songs and waited for their turn at the Great Gulping Gulch Bridge. The bridge was so narrow that vehicles coming from opposite directions had to take turns driving across.

Whenever the kids saw Rush's car in the distance, they'd yell, "Here comes Rush! He's bearing down fast! Driving full blast!"

Then, BLAAAAAAAAT! Rush's horn would blare as he sped past, while the kids shouted reports on the ridiculous things he was doing while driving. "Rush Hotfoot is brushing his teeth!" they'd say.

Or, "Rush Hotfoot is shaving!"
Or, "Rush Hotfoot is plucking his nose hairs!"
Axle Annie would shake her head and warn the kids to be extra careful getting on and off the bus.

One day as Annie approached a railroad crossing, the kids called out their usual warning. "Here comes Rush! Bearing down fast! Driving full blast!"

BLAAAAAAAAT! went Rush's horn when he saw Annie's flashing lights. SCREEEEEEEECH! went his brakes when her stop-sign arm swung out.

"Move that bus," he bellowed, "or I'll move it for you!"

Then, just before Tiger Hill, Rush zoomed past. The kids saw him changing out of his pajamas into his work clothes. "We see London, we see France!" they chanted.

"Don't tell me," groaned Annie.

"Purple underpants!" they cried.

That speed grump made Annie grumpy too! So grumpy that she did something she thought she never would: She attended a meeting of the Burskyville Grouch and Grump Club. And whom should she meet there but Rush Hotfoot himself.

"What do YOU have to be grumpy about?" he asked her with a scowl.

"I'm grumpy about you, Rush Hotfoot. You ruin my mornings."

"Oh no," argued Rush. "Your BUS ruins MY mornings with its flashing lights and stupid stop-sign arm. Your KIDS ruin MY mornings with their sappy singing!"

The other grouches told Axle Annie that she wasn't grumpy enough for them. Being grumpy about Rush Hotfoot didn't count, because Rush Hotfoot would make ANY-BODY grumpy! They all drank a gripe-juice toast to him: "Three cheers for Rush! Hiss-Hiss-Boo! The best bus driver in Burskyville got grumpy because of you!"

The next day a kid with a sprained ankle was struggling onto Annie's bus when he heard a familiar rumble. "Watch out for Rush, Annie," he said. "He's bearing down fast! Driving full blast!"

"I've got two hands on the wheel and nerves of steel," Annie replied. "I always watch out for that speed grump!"

But while Annie's lights were still flashing and her stop-sign arm was still out, Rush Hotfoot roared past the bus. His wheels spat gravel.

Axle Annie was outraged. "Rush Hotfoot is worse than a speed grump," she muttered. "He is a major danger! This time he broke the law."

She radioed her supervisor, who called the police, and soon Rush was pulled over by an officer. Just as the police officer wrote up a ticket for Rush, Axle Annie drove by, her kids singing merrily.

Now Rush Hotfoot was grumpier than ever. He caught up with Annie's bus again halfway up Tiger Hill.

"Watch out, Annie," warned the kids. "Here comes Rush!"

"He can't pass on a hill," said Annie.

But Rush blasted past Annie's bus, up and over Tiger Hill, and on toward the Great Gulping Gulch Bridge. "He was drinking coffee!" yelled Annie's kids.

Rush saw a truck approaching the bridge from the opposite direction. He was in too big a hurry to wait for his turn to cross, so he sped up to beat the truck. Just then his cell phone rang. He reached for it and knocked hot coffee into his lap. "Yeeeeeeowwwwwww!" he shrieked.

Rush's car spun out of control.

SCREEEEEEEECH! BONKETY-BONK-BONK! Rush's car bounced off a guardrail on one side of the bridge, then . . .

CR-R-R-ASH! It smashed into the other side.

When Axle Annie arrived at the bridge, she saw Rush's car, tangled in the railing, dangling over Great Gulping Gulch. Rush was holding on for dear life.

Annie saw the truck approaching from the other direction. What if the truck driver didn't notice Rush's car? What if he smashed into the car and sent it hurtling down into Great Gulping Gulch? She had to figure out a way to save Rush!

Annie maneuvered her bus as close to Rush's car as she could without endangering her kids. She turned on her hazard lights and her white strobe light and her red emergency lights. Her stop-sign arm swung out automatically, and Annie blared her horn while the kids yelled out their windows to the truck driver.

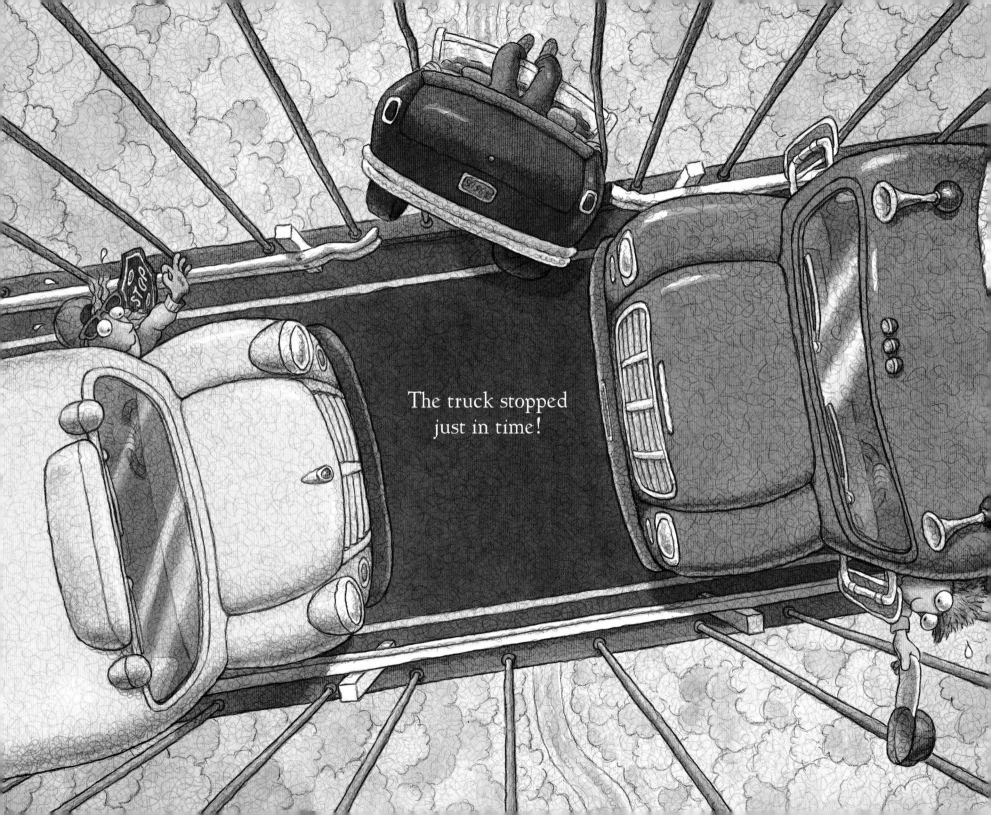

The truck stopped
just in time!

It took two tow trucks and an emergency helicopter to rescue Rush Hotfoot.

Annie's kids sang their favorite songs to him while he waited, to take his mind off being scared.

Rush's car was a wreck, and he lost his driver's license. From then on, he rode a tricycle to work. He wore a safety helmet with flashing lights and a special swing-out stop-sign arm. Everybody had to slow down for Rush Hotfoot.

Rush thought the safest place to be was behind Axle Annie's big yellow bus. After all, Axle Annie had both hands on the wheel and nerves of steel, and she always watched out for speed grumps.